# Arthur's Hall The Doge and the Dogaressa

# By

# E. T. A. Hoffmann

**British Library Cataloguing-in-Publication Data**
A catalogue record for this book is available from the
British Library

# E. T. A. Hoffman

Ernst Theodor Wilhelm Hoffmann was born in Königsberg, East Prussia in 1776. His family were all jurists, and during his youth he was initially encouraged to pursue a career in law. However, in his late teens Hoffman became increasingly interested in literature and philosophy, and spent much of his time reading German classicists and attending lectures by, amongst others, Immanuel Kant.

In was in his twenties, upon moving with his uncle to Berlin, that Hoffman first began to promote himself as a composer, writing an operetta called Die Maske and entering a number of playwriting competitions. Hoffman struggled to establish himself anywhere for a while, flitting between a number of cities and dodging the attentions of Napoleon's occupying troops. In 1808, while living in Bamberg, he began his job as a theatre manager and a music critic, and Hoffman's break came a year later, with the publication of Ritter Gluck. The story centred on a man who meets, or thinks he has met, a long-dead composer, and played into the 'doppelgänger' theme – at that time very popular in literature. It was shortly after this that Hoffman began to use the pseudonym E. T. A. Hoffmann, declaring the 'A' to stand for 'Amadeus', as a tribute to the great composer, Mozart.

Over the next decade, while moving between Dresden, Leipzig and Berlin, Hoffman produced a great range of both literary and musical works. Probably Hoffman's most well-known story, produced in 1816, is 'The Nutcracker and the Mouse King', due to the fact that – some seventy-six years later - it inspired Tchaikovsky's ballet The Nutcracker.

In the same vein, his story 'The Sandman' provided both the inspiration for Léo Delibes's ballet Coppélia, and the basis for a highly influential essay by Sigmund Freud, called 'The Uncanny'. (Indeed, Freud referred to Hoffman as the "unrivalled master of the uncanny in literature.")

Alcohol abuse and syphilis eventually took a great toll on Hoffman though, and – having spent the last year of his life paralysed – he died in Berlin in 1822, aged just 46. His legacy is a powerful one, however: He is seen as a pioneer of both Romanticism and fantasy literature, and his novella, Mademoiselle de Scudéri: A Tale from the Times of Louis XIV is often cited as the first ever detective story.

# The Doge
## and the Dogaressa

**This** was the title that distinguished in the art-catalogue of the works exhibited by the Berlin Academy of Arts in September, 1816, a picture which came from the brush of the skilful clever Associate of the Academy, C. Kolbe.2 There was such a peculiar charm in the piece that it attracted all observers. A Doge, richly and magnificently dressed, and a Dogess at his side, as richly adorned with jewellery, are stepping out on to a balustered balcony; he is an old man, with a grey beard and rusty red face, his features indicating a peculiar blending of expressions, now revealing strength, now weakness, again pride and arrogance, and again pure good-nature; she is a young woman, with a far-away look of yearning sadness and dreamy aspiration not only in her eyes but also in her general bearing. Behind them is an elderly lady and a man holding an open sun-shade. At one end of the balcony is a young man blowing a conch-shaped horn, whilst in front of it a richly decorated gondola, bearing the Venetian flag and having two gondoliers, is rocking on the sea. In the background stretches the sea itself studded with hundreds and hundreds of sails, whilst the towers and palaces of magnificent Venice are seen rising out of its waves. To the left is Saint Mark's, to the right, more in the front, San Giorgio Maggiore. The following words were cut in the golden frame of the picture.

Ah! senza amare,
Andare sul mare
Col sposo del mare,
Non puo consolare.
To go on the sea
With the spouse of the sea,
When loveless I be,
Is no comfort to me.

One day there arose before this picture a fruitless altercation as to whether the artist really intended it for anything more than a mere picture, that is, the temporary situation, sufficiently indicated by the verse, of a decrepit old man who with all his splendour and magnificence is unable to satisfy the desires of a heart filled with yearning aspirations, or whether he intended to represent an actual historical event. One after the other the visitors left the place, tired of the discussion, so that at length there were only two men left, both very good friends to the noble art of painting. "I can't understand," said one of them, "how people can spoil all their enjoyment by eternally hunting after some jejune interpretation or explanation. Independently of the fact that I have a pretty accurate notion of what the relations in life between this Doge and Dogess were, I am more particularly struck by the subdued richness and power that characterises the picture as a whole. Look at this flag with the winged lions, how they flutter in the breeze as if they swayed the world. O beautiful Venice!" He began to recite Turandot's3 riddle of Lion of the Adriatic, "Dimmi, qual sia quella terribil fera," &c. He had hardly come to the end when a sonorous masculine voice broke in with Calaf's4 solution, "Tu quadrupede fera," &c. Unobserved by the friends, a man of tall and noble appearance, his grey mantle thrown picturesquely across his shoulder, had taken up a position behind them, and was examining the picture with sparkling eyes. They got into conversation, and the stranger said almost in atone of solemnity, "It is indeed a singular mystery, how a picture often arises in the mind of an artist, the figures of which, previously indistinguishable, incorporate mist driving about in empty space, first seem to shape themselves into vitality in his mind, and there seem to find their home. Suddenly the picture connects itself with the past, or even with the future, representing something that has really happened or that will happen. Perhaps it was not known to Kolbe himself that the persons he was representing in this picture are none other than the Doge Marino Falieri5 and his lady Annunciata."

The stranger paused, but the two friends urgently entreated him to solve for them this riddle as he had solved that of the Lion of the Adriatic. Whereupon he replied, "If you have patience, my inquisitive sirs, I will at once explain the picture to you by telling you Falieri's history. But have you patience? I shall be very circumstantial, for I cannot speak otherwise of things which stand so life-like before my eyes that I seem to have seen them myself. And that may very well be the case, for all historians — amongst whom I happen to be one — are properly a kind of talking ghost of past ages."

The friends accompanied the stranger into a retired room, when, without further preamble, he began as follows:—

It is now a long time ago, and if I mistake not, it was in the month of August, 1354, that the valiant Genoese captain, Paganino Doria6 by name, utterly routed the Venetians and took their town of Parenzo. And his well-manned galleys were now cruising backwards and forwards in the Lagune, close in front of Venice, like ravenous beasts of prey which, goaded by hunger, roam restlessly up and down spying out where they may most safely pounce upon their victims; and both people and seignory were panic-stricken with fear. All the male population, liable to military service, and everybody who could lift an arm, flew to their weapons or seized an oar. The harbour of Saint Nicholas was the gathering-place for the bands. Ships and trees were sunk, and chains riveted to chains, to lock the harbour-mouth against the enemy. Whilst there was heard the rattle of arms and the wild tumult of preparation, and whilst the ponderous masses thundered down into the foaming sea, on the Rialto the agents of the seignory were wiping the cold sweat from their pale brows, and with troubled countenances and hoarse voices offering almost fabulous percentage for ready money, for the straitened republic was in want of this necessary also. Moreover, it was determined by the inscrutable decree of Providence that just at this period of extreme distress and anxiety, the faithful shepherd should be taken away from his troubled flock. Completely borne down by the burden of the public calamity, the Doge Andrea Dandolo7 died; the people called him the "dear good count" (il caro contino ), because he was always cordial and kind, and never crossed Saint Mark's Square without speaking a word of comfort to those in need of good advice, or giving a few sequins8 to those who were in want of money. And as every blow is wont to fall with double sharpness upon those who are discouraged by misfortune, when at other times they would hardly have felt it at all, so now, when the people heard the bells of Saint Mark's proclaim in solemn muffled tones the death of their Duke, they were utterly undone with sorrow and grief. Their support, their hope, was now gone, and they would have to bend their necks to the Genoese yoke, they cried, in despite of the fact that Dandolo's loss did not seem to have any very counteractive effect upon the progress that was being made with all necessary warlike preparations. The "dear good count" had loved to live in peace and quietness, preferring to follow the wondrous courses of the stars rather than the problematical complications of state policy; he understood how to arrange a procession on Easter Day better than how to lead an army.

The object now was to elect a Doge who, endowed at one and the same time with the valour and genius of a war captain, and with skill in statecraft, should save Venice, now tottering on her foundations, from the threatening power of her bold and ever-bolder enemy. But when the senators assembled there was none but what had a gloomy face, hopeless looks, and head bent earthwards and resting on his supporting hand. Where were they to find a man who could seize the unguided helm and direct the bark of the state aright? At last the oldest of the councillors, called Marino Bodoeri, lifted up his voice and said, "You will not find him here around us, or amongst us; direct your eyes to Avignon, upon Marino Falieri, whom we sent to congratulate Pope Innocent9 on his elevation to the Papal dignity; he can find better work to do now; he's the man for us; let us choose him Doge to stem this current of adversity. You will urge by way of objection that he is now almost eighty years old, that his hair and beard are white as silver, that his blithe appearance, fiery eye, and the deep red of his nose and cheeks are to be ascribed, as his traducers maintain, to good Cyprus wine rather than to energy of character; but heed not that. Remember what conspicuous bravery this Marino Falieri showed as admiral of the fleet in the Black Sea, and bear in mind the great services which prevailed with the Procurators of Saint Mark to invest this Falieri with the rich countship of Valdemarino." Thus highly did Bodoeri extol Falieri's virtues; and he had a ready answer for all objections, so that at length all voices were unanimous in electing Falieri. Several, however, still continued to allude to his hot, passionate temper, his ambition, and his self-will; but they were met with the reply: "And it is exactly because all these have gone from the old man, that we choose the grey-beard Falieri and not the youth Falieri." And these censuring voices were completely silenced when the people, learning upon whom the choice had fallen, greeted it with the loudest and most extravagant demonstrations of delight. Do we not know that in such dangerous times, in times of such tension and unrest, any resolution that really is a resolution is accepted as an inspiration from Heaven? Thus it came to pass that the "dear good count" and all his gentleness and piety were forgotten, and every one cried, "By Saint Mark, this Marino ought long ago to have been our Doge, and then we should not have yon arrogant Doria before our very doors." And crippled soldiers painfully lifted up their wounded arms and cried, "That is Falieri who beat the Morbassan10 — the valiant captain whose victorious banners waved in the Black Sea." Wherever a knot of people gathered, there was one amongst them telling of Falieri's heroic deeds; and, as though Doria were already defeated, the air rang with wild shouts of triumph. An additional reason for this was that Nicolo Pisani11 who, Heaven knows why! instead of going to meet Doria with his fleet, had coolly sailed away to Sardinia,12 was now returned. Doria withdrew from the Lagune; and what was really due to the approach of Pisani's fleet was ascribed to the formidable name of Marino Falieri. Then the people and the seignory were seized by a kind of frantic ecstasy that such an auspicious choice had been made; and as an uncommon way of testifying the same, it was determined to welcome the newly elected Doge as if he were a messenger from heaven bringing honour, victory, and abundance of riches. Twelve nobles, each accompanied by a numerous retinue in rich dresses, had been sent by the Seignory to Verona, where the ambassadors of the Republic were again to announce to Falieri, on his arrival, with all due ceremony, his elevation to the supreme office in the state. Then fifteen richly decorated vessels of state, equipped by the Podesta13 of Chioggia, and under the command of his own son Taddeo Giustiniani, took the Doge and his attendant company on board at Chiozza; and now they moved on like the triumphal procession of a most mighty and victorious monarch to St. Clement's, where the Bucentaur14 was awaiting the Doge.

At this very moment, namely, when Marino Falieri was about to set foot on board the Bucentaur,— and that was on the evening of the 3d of October about sunset — a poor unfortunate man lay stretched at full length on the hard marble pavement in front of the Customhouse. A few rags of striped linen, of a colour now no longer recognisable, the remains of what apparently had once been a sailor's dress, such as was worn by the very poorest of the people — porters and assistant oarsmen, hung about his lean starved body. There was not a trace of a shirt to be seen, except the poor fellow's own skin, which peeped through his rags almost everywhere, and was so white and delicate that the very noblest need not have been shy or ashamed of it Accordingly, his leanness only served to display more fully the perfect proportions of his well-knit frame. A careful scrutiny of the unfortunate's light-chestnut hair, now hanging all tangled and dishevelled about his exquisitely beautiful forehead, his blue eyes dimmed with extreme misery, his Roman nose, his fine formed lips — he seemed to be not more than twenty years old at the most — inevitably suggested that he was of good birth, and had by some adverse turn of fortune been thrown amongst the meanest classes of the people.

As remarked, the youth lay in front of the pillars of the Custom-house, his head resting on his right arm, and his eyes riveted in a vacant stare upon the sea, without movement or change of posture. An observer might well have fancied that he was devoid of life, or that death had fixed him there whilst turning him into an image of stone, had not a deep sigh escaped him from time to time, as if wrung from him by unutterable pain. And they were in fact occasioned by the pain of his left arm, which had apparently been seriously wounded, and was lying stretched out on the pavement, wrapped up in bloody rags.

All labour had ceased; the hum of trade was no longer heard; all Venice, in thousands of boats and gondolas, was gone out to meet the much-lauded Falieri. Hence it was that the unhappy youth was sighing away his pain in utter helplessness. But just as his weary head fell back upon the pavement, and he seemed on the point of fainting, a hoarse and very querulous voice cried several times in succession, "Antonio, my dear Antonio." At length Antonio painfully raised himself partly up; and, turning his head towards the pillars of the Custom-house, whence the voice seemed to proceed, he replied very faintly, and in a scarce intelligible voice, "Who is calling me? Who has come to cast my dead body into the sea, for it will soon be all over with me."

Then a little shrivelled wrinkled crone came up panting and coughing, hobbling along by the aid of her staff; she approached the wounded youth, and squatting down beside him, she burst out into a most repulsive chuckling and laughing. "You foolish child, you foolish child," whispered the old woman, "are you going to perish here — will you stay here to die, while a golden fortune is waiting for you? Look yonder, look yonder at yon blazing fire in the west; there are sequins for you! But you must eat, dear Antonio, eat and drink; for it's only hunger which has made you fall down here on this cold pavement. Your arm is now quite well again, yes, that it is." Antonio recognised in the old crone the singular beggar-woman who was generally to be seen on the steps of the Franciscan Church, chuckling to herself and laughing, and soliciting alms from the worshippers; he himself, urged by some inward inexplicable propensity, had often thrown her a hard-earned penny, which he had not had to spare. "Leave me, leave me in peace, you insane old woman," he said; "but you are right, it is hunger more than my wound which has made me weak and miserable; for three days I have not earned a farthing. I wanted to go over to the monastery15 and see if I could get a spoonful or two of the soup that is made for invalids; but all my companions have gone; there is not one to have compassion upon me and take me in his barca;16 and now I have fallen down here, and shall, I expect, never get up again." "Hi! hi! hi! hi!" chuckled the old woman; "why do you begin to despair so soon? Why lose heart so quickly? You are thirsty and hungry, but I can help you. Here are a few fine dried fish which I bought only today in the Mint; here is lemon-juice and a piece of nice white bread; eat, my son; and then we will look at the wounded arm." And the old woman proceeded to bring forth fish, bread, and lemon juice from the bag which hung like a hood down her back, and also projected right above her bent head. As soon as Antonio had moistened his parched and burning lips with the cool drink, he felt the pangs of hunger return with double fury, and he greedily devoured the bread and the fish.

Meanwhile the old woman was busy unwrapping the rags from his wounded arm, and it was found that, though it was badly crushed, the wound was progressing favourably towards healing. The old woman took a salve out of a little box and warmed it with the breath of her mouth, and as she rubbed it on the wound she asked, "But who then has given you such a nasty blow, my poor boy?" Antonio was so refreshed and charged anew with vital energy that he had raised himself completely up; his eyes flashed, and he shook his doubled fist above his head, crying, "Oh! that rascal Nicolo; he tried to maim me, because he envies me every wretched penny that any generous hand bestows upon me. You know, old dame, that I barely managed to hold body and soul together by helping to carry bales of goods from ships and freight-boats to the dépôt of the Germans, the so-called Fontego17 — of course you know the building"— Directly Antonio uttered the word Fontego, the old woman began to chuckle and laugh most abominably, and to mumble,

"Fontego — Fontego — Fontego." "Have done with your insane laughing if I am to go on with my story," added Antonio angrily. At once the old woman grew quiet, and Antonio continued, "after a time I saved a little bit of money, and bought a new jerkin, so that I looked quite fine; and then I got enrolled amongst the gondoliers. As I was always in a blithe humour, worked hard, and knew a great many good songs, I soon earned a good deal more than the rest. This, however, awakened my comrades' envy. They blackened my character to my master, so that he turned me adrift; and everywhere where I went or where I stood they cried after me, 'German cur! Cursed heretic!' Three days ago, as I was helping to unload a boat near St. Sebastian, they fell upon me with sticks and stones. I defended myself stoutly, but that malicious Nicolo dealt me a blow with his oar, which grazed my head and severely injured my arm, and knocked me on the ground. Ay, you've given me a good meal, old woman, and I am sure I feel that your salve has done my arm a world of good. See, I can already move it easily — now I shall be able to row bravely again." Antonio had risen up from the ground, and was swinging his arm violently backwards and forwards, but the old woman again fell to chuckling and laughing loudly, whilst she hobbled round about him in the most extraordinary fashion — dancing with short tripping steps as it were — and she cried, "My son, my good boy, my good lad — row on bravely — he is coming — he is coming. The gold is shining red in the bright flames. Row on stoutly, row on; but only once more, only once more; and then never again."

But Antonio was not paying the slightest heed to the old woman's words, for the most splendid of spectacles was unfolding itself before his eyes. The Bucentaur, with the Lion of the Adriatic on her fluttering standard, was coming along from St. Clement's to the measured stroke of the oars like a mighty winged golden swan. Surrounded by innumerable barcas and gondolas, and with her head proudly and boldly raised, she appeared like a princess commanding a triumphing army, that had emerged from the depths of the sea, wearing bright and gaily decked helmets. The evening sun was sending down his fiery rays upon the sea and upon Venice, so that everything appeared to have been plunged into a bath of blazing fire; but whilst Antonio, completely forgetful of all his unhappiness, was standing gazing with wonder and delight, the gleams of the sun grew more bloody and more bloody. The wind whistled shrilly and harshly, and a hollow threatening echo came rolling in from the open sea outside. Down burst the storm in the midst of black clouds, and enshrouded all in thick darkness, whilst the waves rose higher and higher, pouring in from the thundering sea like foaming hissing monsters, threatening to engulf everything. The gondolas and barcas were driven in all directions like scattered feathers. The Bucentaur, unable to resist the storm owing to its flat bottom, was yawing from side to side. Instead of the jubilant notes of trumpets and cornets, there was heard through the storm the anxious cries of those in distress.

Antonio gazed upon the scene like one stupefied, without

sense and motion. But then there came a rattling of chains immediately in front of him; he looked down, and saw a little canoe, which was chained to the wall, and was being tossed up and down by the waves; and a thought entered his mind like a flash of lightning. He leaped into the canoe, unfastened it, seized the oar which he found in it, and pushed out boldly and confidently into the sea, directly towards the Bucentaur. The nearer he came to it the more distinctly could he hear shouts for help. "Here, here, come here — save the Doge, save the Doge." It is well known that little fisher-canoes are safer and better to manage in the Lagune when it is stormy than are larger boats; and accordingly these little craft were hastening from all sides to the rescue of Marino Falieri's invaluable person. But it is an invariable principle in life that the Eternal Power reserves every bold deed as a brilliant success to the one specially chosen for it, and hence all others have all their pains for nothing. And as on this occasion it was poor Antonio who was destined to achieve the rescue of the newly elected Doge, he alone succeeded in working his way on to the Bucentaur in his little insignificant fisher-canoe. Old Marino Falieri, familiar with such dangers, stepped firmly, without a moment's hesitation, from the sumptuous but treacherous Bucentaur into poor Antonio's little craft, which, gliding smoothly over the raging waves like a dolphin, brought him in a few minutes to St. Mark's Square. The old man, his clothing saturated with wet, and with large drops of sea-spray in his grey beard, was conducted into the church, where the nobles with blanched faces concluded the ceremonies connected with the Doge's public entry. But the people, as well as the seignory, confounded by this unfortunate contretemps, to which was also added the fact that the Doge, in the hurry and confusion, had been led between the two columns where common malefactors were generally executed, grew silent in the midst of their triumph, and thus the day that had begun in festive fashion ended in gloom and sadness.

Nobody seemed to think about the Doge's rescuer; nor did Antonio himself think about it, for he was lying in the peristyle of the Ducal Palace, half dead with fatigue, and fainting with the pain caused by his wound, which had again burst open. He was therefore all the more surprised when just before midnight a Ducal halberdier took him by the shoulders, saying, "Come along, friend," and led him into the palace, where he pushed him into the Duke's chamber. The old man came to meet him with a kindly smile, and said, pointing to a couple of purses lying on the table, "You have borne yourself bravely, my son. Here; take these three thousand sequins, and if you want more ask for them; but have the goodness never to come into my presence again." As he said these last words the old man's eyes flashed with fire, and the tip of his nose grew a darker red Antonio could not fathom the old man's mind; he did not, however, trouble himself overmuch about it, but with some little difficulty took up the purses, which he believed he had honestly and rightly earned.

Next morning old Falieri, conspicuous in the splendours

21

of his newly acquired dignity, stood in one of the lofty bay windows of the palace, watching the bustling scene below, where the people were busy engaged in practising all kinds of weapons, when Bodoeri, who from the days when he was a youth had enjoyed the intimate and unchangeable friendship of the Doge, entered the apartment. As, however, the Doge was quite wrapped up in himself and his dignity, and did not appear to notice his entrance, Bodoeri clapped his hands together and cried with a loud laugh, "Come, Falieri, what are all these sublime thoughts that are being hatched and nourished in your mind since you first put the Doge's bent bonnet on?" Falieri, coming to himself like one awakening from a dream, stepped forward to meet his old friend with an air of forced amiability. He felt that he really owed his bonnet to Bodoeri, and the words of the latter seemed to be a reminder of the fact. But since every obligation weighed like a burden upon Falieri's proud ambitious spirit, and he could not dismiss the oldest member of the Council, and his tried friend to boot, as he had dismissed poor Antonio, he constrained himself to utter a few words of thanks, and immediately began to speak of the measures to be adopted to meet their enemy, who was now developing so great an activity in every direction. Bodoeri interrupted him and said, cunningly smiling, "That, and all else that the state demands of you, we will maturely weigh and consider an hour or two hence in a full meeting of the Great Council. I have not come to you thus early in order to invent a plan for defeating yon presumptuous Doria or bringing to reason Louis18 the

22

Hungarian, who is again setting his longing eyes upon our Dalmatian seaports. No, Marino, I was thinking solely about you, and about what you perhaps would not guess — your marriage." "How came you to think of such a thing as that?" replied the Doge, greatly annoyed; and rising to his feet, he turned his back upon Bodoeri and looked out of the window. "It's a long time to Ascension Day. By that time I hope the enemy will be routed, and that victory, honour, additional riches, and a wider extension of power will have been won for the sea-born lion of the Adriatic. The chaste bride shall find her bridegroom worthy of her." "Pshaw! pshaw!" interrupted Bodoeri, impatiently; "you are talking about that memorable ceremony on Ascension Day, when you will throw the gold ring from the Bucentaur into the waves under the impression that you are wedding the Adriatic Sea. But do you not know,— you, Marino, you, kinsman to the sea,— of any other bride than the cold, damp, treacherous element which you delude yourself into the belief that you rule, and which only yesterday revolted against you in such dangerous fashion? Marry, how can you fancy lying in the arms of such a bride of such a wild, wayward thing? Why when you only just skimmed her lips as you rode along in the Bucentaur she at once began to rage and storm. Would an entire Vesuvius of fiery passion suffice to warm the icy bosom of such a false bride as that? Continually faithless, she is wedded time after time, nor does she receive the ring as a treasured symbol of love, but she extorts it as a tribute from a slave? No, Marino, I was thinking of your marriage to the most beautiful child of the earth than can be found." "You are prating utter nonsense, utter nonsense, I tell you, old man," murmured Falieri without turning away from the window. "I, a grey-haired old man, eighty years of age, burdened with toil and trouble, who have never been married, and now hardly capable of loving"—— "Stop," cried Bodoeri, "don't slander yourself. Does not the Winter, however rough and cold he may be, at last stretch out his longing arms towards the beautiful goddess who comes to meet him borne by balmy western winds? And when he presses her to his benumbed bosom, when a gentle glow pervades his veins, where then is his ice and his snow? You say you are eighty years old; that is true; but do you measure old age then by years merely? Don't you carry your head as erect and walk with as firm a step as you did forty summers ago? Or do you perhaps feel that your strength is failing you, that you must carry a lighter sword, that you grow faint when you walk fast, or get short of breath when you ascend the steps of the Ducal Palace?" "No, by Heaven, no," broke in Falieri upon his friend, as he turned away from the window with an abrupt passionate movement and approached him, "no, I feel no traces of age upon me." "Well then," continued Bodoeri, "take deep draughts in your old age of all the delights of earth which are now destined for you. Elevate the woman whom I have chosen for you to be your Dogess; and then all the ladies of Venice will be constrained to admit that she stands first of all in beauty and in virtue, even as the Venetians recognise in you their captain in valour, intellect, and power."

Bodoeri now began to sketch the picture of a beautiful woman, and in doing so he knew how to mix his colours so cleverly, and lay them on with so much vigour and effect, that old Falieri's eyes began to sparkle, and his face grew redder and redder, whilst he puckered up his mouth and smacked his lips as if he were draining sundry glasses of fiery Syracuse. "But who is this paragon of loveliness of whom you are speaking?" said he at last with a smirk. "I mean nobody else but my dear niece — it's she I mean," replied Bodoeri. "What! your niece?" interrupted Falieri. "Why, she was married to Bertuccio Nenolo when I was Podesta of Treviso." "Oh! you are thinking about my niece Francesca," continued Bodoeri, "but it is her sweet daughter whom I intend for you. You know how rude, rough Nenolo was enticed to the wars and drowned at sea. Francesca buried her pain and grief in a Roman nunnery, and so I had little Annunciata brought up in strict seclusion at my villa in Treviso"—— "What!" cried Falieri, again impatiently interrupting the old man, "you mean me to raise your niece's daughter to the dignity of Dogess? How long is it since Nenolo was married? Annunciata must be a child — at the most only ten years old. When I was Podesta in Treviso, Nenolo had not even thought of marrying, and that's"—— "Twenty-five years ago," interposed Bodoeri, laughing; "come, you are getting all at sea with your memory of the flight of time, it goes so rapidly with you. Annunciata is a maiden of nineteen, beautiful as the sun, modest, submissive, inexperienced in love, for she has hardly ever seen a man. She will cling to you with childlike affection and unassuming devotion." "I will see her, I will see her," exclaimed the Doge, whose eyes again beheld the picture of the beautiful Annunciata which Bodoeri had sketched.

His desire was gratified the self-same day; for immediately he got back to his own apartments from the meeting of the Great Council, the crafty Bodoeri, who no doubt had many reasons for wishing to see his niece Dogess at Falieri's side, brought the lovely Annunciata to him secretly. Now, when old Falieri saw the angelic maiden, he was quite taken aback by her wonderful beauty, and was scarcely able to stammer out a few unintelligible words as he sued for her hand. Annunciata, no doubt well instructed by Bodoeri beforehand, fell upon her knees before the princely old man, her cheeks flushing crimson. She grasped his hand and pressed it to her lips, softly whispering, "O sir, will you indeed honour me by raising me to a place at your side on your princely throne? Oh! then I will reverence you from the depths of my soul, and will continue your faithful handmaiden as long as I have breath." Old Falieri was beside himself with happiness and delight. As Annunciata took his hand he felt a convulsive throb in every limb; and then his head and all his body began to tremble and totter to such a degree that he had to sink hurriedly into his great arm-chair. It seemed as if he were about to refute Bodoeri's good opinion as to the strength and toughness of his eighty summers. Bodoeri, in fact, could not keep back the peculiar smile that darted across his lips; innocent, un sophisticated Annunciata observed nothing;

26

and happily no one else was present Finally it was resolved for some reason — either because old Falieri felt in what an uncomfortable position he would appear in the eyes of the people as the betrothed of a maiden of nineteen, or because it occurred to him as a sort of presentiment that the Venetians, who were so prone to mockery, ought not to be so directly challenged to indulge in it, or because he deemed it better to say nothing at all about the critical period of betrothal — at any rate, it was resolved, with Bodoeri's consent, that the marriage should be celebrated with the greatest secrecy, and that then some days later the Dogess should be introduced to the seignory and the people as if she had been some time married to Falieri, and had just arrived from Treviso, where she had been staying during Falieri's mission to Avignon.

Let us now turn our eyes upon yon neatly dressed handsome youth who is going up and down the Rialto with his purse of sequins in his hand, conversing with Jews, Turks, Armenians, Greeks.19 He turns away his face with a frown, walks on further, stands still, turns round, and ultimately has himself rowed by a gondolier to St. Mark's Square. There he walks up and down with uncertain hesitating steps, his arms folded and his eyes bent upon the ground; nor does he observe, or even have any idea, that all the whispering and low coughing from various windows and various richly draped balconies are love-signals which are meant for him. Who would have easily recognised in this youth the same Antonio who a few days before had lain on the marble pavement in front of the Custom-house, poor, ragged, and miserable?

"My dear boy! My dear golden boy, Antonio, good day, good day!" Thus he was greeted by the old beggar-woman, who sat on the steps leading to St. Mark's Church, and whom he was going past without observing. Turning abruptly round, he recognised the old woman, and, dipping his hand into his purse, took out a handful of sequins with the intention of throwing them to her. "Oh! keep your gold in your purse," chuckled and laughed the old woman; "what should I do with your money? am I not rich enough? But if you want to do me a kindness, get me a new hood made, for this which I am now wearing is no longer any protection against wind and weather. Yes, please get me one, my dear boy, my dear golden boy,— but keep away from the Fontego,— keep away from the Fontego." Antonio stared into the old woman's pale yellow face, the deep wrinkles in which twitched convulsively in a strange awe-inspiring way. And when she clapped her lean bony hands together so that the joints cracked, and continued her disagreeable laugh, and went on repeating in a hoarse voice, "Keep away from the Fontego," Antonio cried, "Can you not have done with that mad insane nonsense, you old witch?"

As Antonio uttered this word, the old woman, as if struck by a lightning-flash, came rolling down the high marble steps like a ball. Antonio leapt forward and grasped her by both hands, and so prevented her from falling heavily. "O my good lad, my good lad," said the old crone in a low, querulous voice, "what a hideous word that was which you uttered. Kill me rather than repeat that word to me again.

28

Oh! you don't know how deeply you have cut me to the heart, me — who have such a true affection for you — no, you don't know"—— Abruptly breaking off, she wrapped up her head in the dark brown cloth flaps which covered her shoulders like a short mantle, and sighed and moaned as if suffering unspeakable pain. Antonio felt his heart strangely moved; lifting up the old woman, he carried her up into the vestibule of the church, and set her down upon one of the marble benches which were there. "You have been kind to me, old woman," he began, after he had liberated her head from the ugly cloth flaps, "you have been kind to me, since it is to you that I really owe all my prosperity; for if you had not stood by me in the hour of need, I should long ere this have been at the bottom of the sea, nor should I have rescued the old Doge, and received these good sequins. But even if you had not shown that kindness to me, I yet feel that I should have a special liking for you as long as I live, in spite of the fact that your insane behaviour — chuckling and laughing so horribly — strikes my heart with awe. To tell you the truth, old dame, even when I had hard work to get a living by carrying merchandise and rowing, I always felt as if I must work still harder that I might have a few pence to give you." "O son of my heart, my golden Tonino," cried the old woman, raising her shrivelled arms above her head, whilst her staff fell rattling on the marble floor and rolled away from her, "O Tonino mine, I know it; yes, I know it; you must cling to me with all your soul, you may do as you will, for — but hush! hush! hush!" The old woman stooped painfully down in order to reach her staff, but Antonio picked it up and handed it to her.

Leaning her sharp chin on her staff, and riveting her eyes in a set stare upon the ground, she began to speak in a reserved but hollow voice, "Tell me, my child, have you no recollection at all of any former time, of what you did or where you were before you found yourself here, a poor wretch hardly able to keep body and soul together?" With a deep sigh, Antonio took his seat beside the old crone and then began, "Alas! mother, only too well do I know that I was born of parents living in the most prosperous circumstances; but who they were and how I came to leave them, of this I have not the slightest notion, nor could I have. I remember very well a tall handsome man, who often took me in his arms and smothered me with kisses and put sweets in my mouth. And I can also in the same way call to mind a pleasant and pretty lady, who used to dress and undress me and place me in a soft little bed every night, and who in fact was very kind to me in every way. They used to talk to me in a foreign, sonorous language, and I also stammered several words of the same tongue after them. Whilst I was an oarsman my jealous rivals used to say I must be of German origin, from the colour of my hair and eyes, and from my general build. And this I believe myself, for the language which that man spoke (he must have been my father) was German. But the most vivid recollection which I have of that time is that of one terrible night, when I was awakened out of deep sleep by a fearful scream of distress. People were running about the house; doors were being opened and banged to; I grew terribly frightened, and began to cry loudly. Then the lady who used to dress me and take care of me burst into the room, snatched me out of bed, stopped my mouth, enveloped me in shawls, and ran off with me. From that moment I can remember nothing more, until I found myself again in a splendid house, situated in a most charming district. Then there rises up the image of a man whom I called 'father,' a majestic man of noble but benevolent appearance. Like all the rest in the house, he spoke Italian.

"For several weeks I had not seen my father, when one day several ugly-looking strangers came and kicked up a great deal of noise in the house, rummaging about and turning out everything. When they saw me they asked who I was, and what I was doing there? 'Don't you know I'm Antonio, and belong to the house?' I replied; but they laughed in my face and tore off all my fine clothes and turned me out of doors, threatening to have me whipped if I dared to show myself again. I ran away screaming and crying. I had not gone a hundred yards from the house when I met an old man, whom I recognised as being one of my foster-father's servants. 'Come along, Antonio,' he said, taking hold of my hand, 'come along, my poor boy, that house is now closed to us both for ever. We must both look out and see how we can earn a crust of bread.'

"The old man brought me along with him here. He was not so poor as he seemed to be from his mean clothing. Directly we arrived I saw him rip up his jerkin and produce a bag of sequins; and he spent the whole day running about on the Rialto, now acting as broker, now dealing on his own account. I had always to be close at his heels; and whenever he had made a bargain he had a habit of begging a trifle for the figliuolo (little boy). Every one whom I looked boldly in the face was glad to pull out a few pence, which the old man pocketed with infinite satisfaction, affirming, as he stroked my cheeks, that he was saving it up to buy me a new jerkin. I was very comfortable with the old man, whom the people called Old Father Bluenose, though for what reason I don't know. But this life did not last long. You will remember that terrible time, old woman, when one day the earth began to tremble, and towers and palaces were shaken to their very foundations and began to reel and totter, and the bells to ring as if tolled by the arms of invisible giants. Hardly seven years have passed since that day. Fortunately I escaped along with my old man out of the house before it fell in with a crash behind us. There was no business doing; everybody on the Rialto seemed stunned, and everything lifeless. But this dreadful event was only the precursor of another approaching monster, which soon breathed out its poisonous breath over the town and the surrounding country. It was known that the pestilence, which had first made its way from the Levant into Sicily, was committing havoc in Tuscany.20 As yet Venice had been spared. One day Old Father Bluenose was dealing with an Armenian on the Rialto; they were agreed over their bargain, and warmly shook hands. Father Bluenose had sold the Armenian certain good wares at a very low price, and now asked for the usual trifle for the figliuolo. The stranger, a big stalwart man with a thick curly beard (I can see him now), bent a kind look upon me, and then kissed me, pressing a few sequins into my hand, which I hastily pocketed. We took a gondola to St. Mark's. On the way the old man asked me for the sequins, but for some reason or other, I don't know what induced me to do it, I maintained that I must keep them myself, since the Armenian had wished me to do so. The old man got angry; but whilst he was quarrelling with me I noticed a disagreeable dirty yellow colour spreading over his face, and that he was mixing up all sorts of incoherent nonsense in his talk. When we reached the Square he reeled about like a drunken man, until he fell to the ground in front of the Ducal Palace — dead. With a loud wail I threw myself upon the corpse. The people came running round us, but as soon as the dreaded cry 'The pestilence! the pestilence!' was heard, they scattered and flew apart in terror. At the same moment I was seized by a dull numbing pain, and my senses left me.

"When I awoke I found I was in a spacious room, lying on a plain mattress, and covered with a blanket. Round about me there were fully twenty or thirty other pale ghastly forms lying on similar mattresses. As I learned later, certain compassionate monks, who happened to be just coming out of St. Mark's, had, on finding signs of life in me, put me in a gondola and got me taken over to Giudecca into the monastery of San Giorgio Maggiore, where the Benedictines had established a hospital. How can I describe to you, old woman, this moment of reawakening? The violence of the plague had completely robbed me of all recollections of the past. Just as if the spark of life had been suddenly dropped into a lifeless statue, I had but a momentary kind of existence, so to speak, linked on to nothing. You may imagine what trouble, what distress this life occasioned me in which my consciousness seemed to swim in empty space without an anchorage. All that the monks could tell me was that I had been found beside Father Bluenose, whose son I was generally accounted to be. Gradually and slowly I gathered my thoughts together, and tried to reflect upon my previous life, but what I have told you, old dame, is all that I can remember of it, and that consists only of certain individual disconnected pictures. Oh! this miserable being-alone-inthe-world! I can't be gay and happy, no matter what may happen!" "Tonino, my dear Tonino," said the old woman, "be contented with what the present moment gives you."

"Say no more, old woman, say no more," interrupted Antonio; "there is still something else which embitters my life, following me about incessantly everywhere; I know it will be the utter ruin of me in the end. An unspeakable longing,— a consuming aspiration for something,— I can neither say nor even conceive what it is — has taken complete possession of my heart and mind since I awoke to renewed life in the hospital. Whilst I was still poor and wretched, and threw myself down at night on my hard couch, weary and worn out by the hard heavy labour of the day, a dream used to come to me, and, fanning my hot brow with balmy rustling breezes, shed about my heart all the inexpressible bliss of some single happy moment, in which the Eternal Power had been pleased to grant me in thought a glimpse of the delights of heaven, and the memory of which was treasured up in the recesses of my soul I now rest on soft cushions, and no labour consumes my strength: but if I awaken out of a dream, or if in my waking hours the recollection of that great moment returns to my mind, I feel that the lonely wretched existence I lead is just as much an oppressive burden now as it was then, and that it is vain for me to try and shake it off. All my thinking and all my inquiries are fruitless; I cannot fathom what this glorious thing is which formerly happened in my life. Its mysterious and alas! to me, unintelligible echo, as it were, fills me with such great happiness; but will not this happiness pass over into the most agonising pain, and torture me to death, when I am obliged to acknowledge that all my hope of ever finding that unknown Eden again, nay, that even the courage to search for it, is lost? Can there indeed remain traces of that which has vanished without leaving any sign behind it?" Antonio ceased speaking, and a deep and painful sigh escaped his breast.

During his narrative the old crone had behaved like one who sympathised fully with his trouble, and felt all that he felt, and like a mirror reflected every movement and gesture which the pain wrung from him. "Tonino," she now began in a tearful voice, "my dear Tonino, do you mean to tell me that you let your courage sink because the remembrance of some glorious moment in your life has perished out of your mind?

You foolish child! You foolish child! Listen to — hi! hi! hi!"
The old woman began to chuckle and laugh in her usual
disagreeable way, and to hop about on the marble floor. Some
people came; she cowered down in her accustomed posture;
they threw her alms. "Antonio — lead me away, Antonio —
away to the sea," she croaked Almost involuntarily — he
could not explain how it came about — he took her by the
arm and led her slowly across St. Mark's Square. On the way
the old woman muttered softly and solemnly, "Antonio, do
you see these dark stains of blood here on the ground? Yes,
blood — much blood — much blood everywhere! But, hi! hi!
hi! Roses will spring up out of the blood — beautiful red roses
for a wreath for you — for your sweetheart. O good Lord of
all, what lovely angel of light is this, who is coming to meet
you with such grace and such a bright starry smile? Her lily-
white arms are stretched out to embrace you. O Antonio, you
lucky, lucky lad! bear yourself bravely! bear yourself bravely!
And at the sweet hour of sunset you may pluck myrtle-leaves
— myrtle-leaves for the bride — for the maiden-widow —
hi! hi! hi! Myrtle-leaves plucked at the hour of sunset, but
these will not be blossoms until midnight! Do you hear the
whisperings of the night-winds? the longing moaning swell
of the sea? Row away bravely, my bold oarsman, row away
bravely!" Antonio's heart was deeply thrilled with awe as
he listened to the old crone's wonderful words, which she
mumbled to herself in a very peculiar and extraordinary way,
mingled with an incessant chuckling.

They came to the pillar which bears the Lion of the

Adriatic. The old woman was going on right past it, still muttering to herself; but Antonio, feeling very uncomfortable at the old crone's behaviour, and being, moreover, stared at in astonishment by the passers-by, stopped and said roughly, "Here — sit you down on these steps, old woman, and have done with your talk; it will drive me mad. It is a fact that you saw my sequins in the fiery images in the clouds; but, for that very reason, what do you mean by prating about angels of light — bride — maiden-widow — roses and myrtle-leaves? Do you want to make a fool of me, you fearful woman, till some insane attempt hurries me to destruction? You shall have a new hood — bread — sequins — all that you want, but leave me alone." And he was about to make off hastily; but the old woman caught him by the mantle, and cried in a shrill piercing voice, "Tonino, my Tonino, do take a good look at me for once, or else I must go to the very edge of the Square yonder and in despair throw myself over into the sea." In order to avoid attracting more eyes upon him than he was already doing, Antonio actually stood still. "Tonino," went on the old woman, "sit down here beside me; my heart is bursting, I must tell you — Oh! do sit down here beside me." Antonio sat down on the steps, but so as to turn his back upon her; and he took out his account-book, whose white pages bore witness to the zeal with which he did business on the Rialto.

The old woman now whispered very low, "Tonino, when you look upon my shrivelled features, does there not dawn upon your mind the slightest, faintest recollection of having known me formerly a long, long time ago?" "I have already told you, old woman," replied Antonio in the same low tones, and without turning round, "I have already told you, that I feel drawn towards you in a way that I can't explain to myself, but I don't attribute it to your ugly shrivelled face. Nay, when I look at your strange black glittering eyes and sharp nose, at your blue lips and long chin, and bristly grey hair, and when I hear your abominable chuckling and laughing, and your confused talk, I rather turn away from you with disgust, and am even inclined to believe that you possess some execrable power for attracting me to you." "O God! God! God!" whined the old dame, a prey to unspeakable pain, "what fiendish spirit of darkness has put such fearful thoughts into your head? O Tonino, my darling Tonino, the woman who took such tender loving care of you when a child, and who saved your life from the most threatening danger on that awful night — it was I."

In the first moments of startled surprise Antonio turned round as if shot; but then he fixed his eyes upon the old woman's hideous face and cried angrily, "So that is the way you think you are going to befool me, you abominable insane old crone! The few recollections which I have retained of my childhood are fresh and lively. That kind and pretty lady who tended me — Oh! I can see her plainly now! She had a full bright face with some colour in it — eyes gently smiling- beautiful dark-brown hair — dainty hands; she could hardly be thirty years old, and you — you, an old woman of ninety!" "O all ye saints of Heaven!" interrupted the old dame, sobbing, "all ye blessed ones, what shall I do to make my Tonino believe in me, his faithful Margaret?" "Margaret!" murmured Antonio, "Margaret! That name falls upon my ears like music heard a long long time ago, and for a long long time forgotten. But — no, it is impossible — impossible." Then the old dame went on more calmly, dropping her eyes, and scribbling as it were with her staff on the ground, "You are right; the tall handsome man who used to take you in his arms and kiss you and give you sweets was your father, Tonino; and the language in which we spoke to each other was the beautiful sonorous German. Your father was a rich and influential merchant in Augsburg. His young and lovely wife died in giving birth to you. Then, since he could not settle down in the place where his dearest lay buried, he came hither to Venice, and brought me, your nurse, with him to take care of you. That terrible night an awful fate overtook your father, and also threatened you. I succeeded in saving you. A noble Venetian adopted you; I, deprived of all means of support, had to remain in Venice.

"My father, a barber-surgeon, of whom it was said that he practised forbidden science as well, had made me familiar from my earliest childhood with the mysterious virtues of Nature's remedies. By him I was taught to wander through the fields and woods, learning the properties of many healing herbs, of many insignificant mosses, the hours when they should be plucked and gathered, and how to mix the juices of the various simples. But to this knowledge there was added a very special gift, which Heaven has endowed me with for some inscrutable purpose. I often see future events as if in a dim and distant mirror; and almost without any conscious effort of will, I declare in expressions which are unintelligible to myself what I have seen; for some unknown Power compels me, and I cannot resist it. Now when I had to stay behind in Venice, deserted of all the world, I resolved to earn a livelihood by means of my tried skill. In a brief time I cured the most dangerous diseases. And furthermore, as my presence alone had a beneficial effect upon my patients, and the soft stroking of my hand often brought them past the crisis in a few minutes, my fame necessarily soon spread through the town, and money came pouring in in streams. This awakened the jealousy of the physicians, quacks who sold their pills and essences in St. Mark's Square, on the Rialto, and in the Mint, poisoning their patients instead of curing them. They spread abroad that I was in league with the devil himself; and they were believed by the superstitious folk. I was soon arrested and brought before the ecclesiastical tribunal. O my Tonino, what horrid tortures did they inflict upon me in order to force from me a confession of the most damnable of all alliances! I remained firm. My hair turned white; my body withered up to a mummy; my feet and hands were paralysed. But there was still the terrible rack left — the cunningest invention of the foul fiend,— and it extorted from me a confession at which I shudder even now. I was to be burnt alive; but when the earthquake shook the foundations of the palaces and of the great prison, the door of the underground dungeon in which I lay confined sprang open of itself, and I staggered up out of my grave as it were through rubbish and ruins.21 O Tonino, you called me an old woman of ninety; I am hardly more than fifty. This lean, emaciated body, this hideously distorted face, this icicle-like hair, these lame feet — no, it was not the lapse of years, it was only unspeakable tortures which could in a few months change me thus from a strong woman into the monstrous creature I now am. And my hideous chuckling and laughing — this was forced from me by the last strain on the rack, at the memory of which my hair even now stands on an end, and I feel altogether as if I were locked in a red-hot coat of mail; and since that time I have been constantly subject to it; it attacks me without my being able to check it. So don't stand any longer in awe of me, Tonino, Oh! it was indeed your heart which told you that as a little boy you lay on my bosom." "Woman," said Antonio hoarsely, wrapped up in his own thoughts, "woman, I feel as if I must believe you. But who was my father? What was he called? What was the awful fate which overtook him on that terrible night? Who was it who adopted me? And — what was that occurrence in my life which now, like some potent magical spell from a strange and unknown world, exercises an irresistible sway over my soul, so that all my thoughts are dissipated into a dark night-like sea, so to speak? When you tell me all this, you mysterious woman, then I will believe you." "Tonino," replied the old crone, sighing, "for your own sake I must keep silent; but the time when I may speak will soon come. The Fontego — the Fontego — keep away from the Fontego."

41

"Oh!" cried Antonio angrily, "you need not begin to speak your dark sentences again to enchant me by some devilish wile or other. My heart is rent, you must speak, or"——— "Stop," interrupted she, "no threats — am I not your faithful nurse, who tended you?"——— Without waiting to hear what the old woman had got further to say, he picked himself up and ran away swiftly. From a distance he shouted to her, "You shall nevertheless have a new hood, and as many sequins besides as you like."

It was in truth a remarkable spectacle, to see the old Doge Marino Falieri and his youthful wife: he, strong enough and robust enough in very truth, but with a grey beard, and innumerable wrinkles in his rusty brown face, with some difficulty bearing his head erect, forming a pathetic figure as he strode along; she, a perfect picture of grace, with the pure gentleness of an angel in her divinely beautiful face, an irresistible charm in her longing glances, a queenly dignity enthroned upon her open lily-white brow, shadowed by her dark locks, a sweet smile upon her cheeks and lips, her pretty head bent with winsome submissiveness, her slender form moving with ease, scarce seeming to touch the earth — a beautiful lady in fact, a native of another and a higher world. Of course you have seen angelic forms like this, conceived and painted by the old masters. Such was Annunciata. How then could it be otherwise but that every one who saw her was astonished and enraptured with her beauty, and all the fiery youths of the Seignory were consumed with passion, measuring the old Doge with mocking looks, and swearing in their hearts that they would be the Mars to this Vulcan, let the consequences be what they might? Annunciata soon found herself surrounded with admirers, to whose flattering and seductive words she listened quietly and graciously, without thinking anything in particular about them. The conception which her pure angelic spirit had formed of her relation to her aged and princely husband was that she ought to honour him as her supreme lord, and cling to him with all the unquestioning fidelity of a submissive handmaiden. He treated her kindly, nay tenderly; he pressed her to his ice-cold heart and called her his darling; he heaped up all the jewels he could find upon her; what else could she wish for from him, what other rights could she have upon him? In this way, therefore, it was impossible for the thought of unfaithfulness to the old man ever in any way to find lodgment in her mind; all that lay beyond the narrow circle of these limited relations was to this good child an unknown region, whose forbidden borders were wrapped in dark mists, unseen and unsuspected by her. Hence all efforts to win her love were fruitless.

But the flames of passion — of love for the beautiful Dogess — burned in none so violently and so uncontrolled as in Michele Steno. Notwithstanding his youth, he was invested with the important and influential post of Member of the Council of Forty. Relying upon this fact, as well as upon his personal beauty, he felt confident of success. Old Marino Falieri he did not fear in the least; and, indeed, the old man seemed to indulge less frequently in his violent outbreaks of furious passion, and to have laid aside his rugged untamable fierceness, since his marriage. There he sat beside his beautiful Annunciata, spruce and prim, in the richest, gayest apparel, smirking and smiling, challenging in the sweet glances of his grey eyes,— from which a treacherous tear stole from time to time,— those who were present to say if any one of them could boast of such a wife as his. Instead of speaking in the rough arrogant tone of voice in which he had formerly been in the habit of expressing himself, he whispered, scarce moving his lips, addressed every one in the most amiable manner, and granted the most absurd petitions. Who would have recognised in this weak amorous old man the same Falieri who had in a fit of passion buffeted the bishop22 on Corpus Christi Day at Treviso, and who had defeated the valiant Morbassan. This growing weakness spurred on Michele Steno to attempt the most extravagant schemes. Annunciata did not understand why he was constantly pursuing her with his looks and words; she had no conception of his real purpose, but always preserved the same gentle, calm, and friendly bearing towards him. It was just this quiet unconscious behaviour, however, which drove him wild, which drove him to despair almost. He determined to effect his end by sinister means. He managed to involve Annunciata's most confidential maid in a love intrigue, and she at last permitted him to visit her at night. Thus he believed he had paved a way to Annunciata's unpolluted chamber; but the Eternal Power willed that this treacherous iniquity should recoil upon the head of its wicked author.

One night it chanced that the Doge, who had just

received the ill tidings of the battle which Nicolo Pisani had lost against Doria off Porto Longo,23 was unable to sleep owing to care and anxiety, and was rambling through the passages of the Ducal Palace. Then he became aware of a shadow stealing apparently out of Annunciata's apartments and creeping towards the stairs. He at once rushed towards it; it was Michele Steno leaving his mistress. A terrible thought flashed across Falieri's mind; with the cry "Annunciata!" he threw himself upon Steno with his drawn dagger in his hand. But Steno, who was stronger and more agile than the old man, averted the thrust, and knocked him down with a violent blow of his fist; then, laughing loudly and shouting, "Annunciata! Annunciata!" he rushed downstairs. The old man picked himself up and stole towards Annunciata's apartments, his heart on fire with the torments of hell. All was quiet, as still as the grave. He knocked; a strange maid opened the door — not the one who was in the habit of sleeping near Annunciata's chamber. "What does my princely husband command at this late and unusual hour?" asked Annunciata in a calm and sweetly gentle tone, for she had meanwhile thrown on a light night-robe and was now come forward. Old Falieri stared at her speechless; then, raising both hands above his head, he cried, "No, it is not possible, it is not possible." "What is not possible, my princely sir?" asked Annunciata, startled at the deep solemn tones of the old man's voice. But Falieri, without answering her question, turned to the maid, "Why are you sleeping here? why does not Luigia sleep here as usual?" "Oh!" replied the little one,

45

"Luigia would make me exchange places with her to-night; she is sleeping in the ante-room close by the stairs." "Close by the stairs!" echoed Falieri, delighted; and he hurried away to the ante-room. At his loud knocking Luigia opened the door; and when she saw the Doge, her master's face inflamed with rage, and his flashing eyes, she threw herself upon her bare knees and confessed her shame, which was set beyond all doubt by a pair of elegant gentleman's gloves lying on the easy-chair, whilst the sweet scent about them betrayed their dandified owner. Hotly incensed at Steno's unheard-of impudence, the Doge wrote to him next morning, forbidding him, on pain of banishment from the town, to approach the Ducal Palace, or the presence of the Doge and Dogess.

Michele Steno was wild with fury at the failure of his well-planned scheme, and at the disgrace of being thus banished from the presence of his idol. Now when he had to see from a distance how gently and kindly the Dogess spoke to other young men of the Seignory — that was indeed her natural manner — his envy and the violence of his passion filled his mind with evil thoughts. The Dogess had without doubt only scorned him because he had been anticipated by others with better luck; and he had the hardihood to utter his thoughts openly and publicly. Now whether it was that old Falieri had tidings of this shameless talk, or whether he came to look upon the occurrence of that memorable night as the warning finger of destiny, or whether now, in spite of all his calmness and equanimity, and his perfect confidence in the fidelity of his wife, he saw clearly the danger of the unnatural position in which he stood in respect to her — at any rate he became ill-tempered and morose. He was plagued and tortured by all the fiends of jealousy, and confined Annunciata to the inner apartments of the Ducal Palace, so that no man ever set eyes upon her. Bodoeri took his niece's part, and soundly rated old Falieri; but he would not hear of any change in his conduct.

All this took place shortly before Holy Thursday. On the occasion of the popular sports which take place on this day in St. Mark's Square, it was customary for the Dogess to take her seat beside the Doge, under a canopy erected on the balcony which lies opposite to the Piazetti. Bodoeri reminded the Doge of this custom, and told him that it would be very absurd, and sure to draw down upon him the mocking laughter of both populace and Seignory, if, in the teeth of custom and usage, he let his perverse jealousy exclude Annunciata from this honour. "Do you think," replied old Falieri, whose pride was immediately aroused, "do you think I am such an idiotic old fool that I am afraid to show my most precious jewel for fear of thievish hands, and that I could not prevent her being stolen from me with my good sword? No, old man, you are mistaken; tomorrow Annunciata shall go with me in solemn procession across St. Mark's Square, that the people may see their Dogess, and on Holy Thursday she shall receive the nosegay from the bold sailor who comes sailing down out of the air to her." The Doge was thinking of a very ancient custom as he said these words. On Holy Thursday a bold fellow from amongst the people is drawn up from the sea to the summit of the tower of St. Mark's, in a machine that resembles a little ship and is suspended on ropes, then he shoots from the top of the tower with the speed of an arrow down to the Square where the Doge and Dogess are sitting, and presents a nosegay of flowers to the Dogess, or to the Doge if he is alone.

The next day the Doge carried out his intention. Annunciata had to don her most magnificent robes; and surrounded by the Seignory and attended by pages and guards, she and Falieri crossed the Square when it was swarming with people. They pushed and squeezed themselves to death almost to see the beautiful Dogess; and he who succeeded in setting eyes upon her thought he had taken a peep into Paradise and had beheld the loveliest of the bright and beautiful angels. But according to Venetian habits, in the midst of the wildest outbreaks of their frantic admiration, here and there were heard all sorts of satiric phrases and rhymes — and coarse enough too — aimed at old Falieri and his young wife. Falieri, however, appeared not to notice them, but strode along as pathetically as possible at Annunciata's side, smirking and smiling all over his face, and free on this occasion from all jealousy, although he must have seen the glances full of burning passion which were directed upon his beautiful lady from all sides. Arrived before the principal entrance to the Palace, the guards had some difficulty in driving back the crowd, so that the Doge and Dogess might go in; but here and there were still standing isolated knots of better-dressed citizens, who could not very well be refused entrance into even the inner quadrangle of the Palace. Now it happened just at the moment that the Dogess entered the quadrangle, that a young man, who with a few others stood under the portico, fell down suddenly upon the hard marble floor, as if dead, with the loud scream, "O good God! good God!" The people ran together from every side and surrounded the dead man, so that the Dogess could not see him; yet, as the young man fell, she felt as if a red-hot knife were suddenly thrust into her heart; she grew pale; she reeled, and was only prevented from fainting by the smelling-bottles of the ladies who hastened to her assistance. Old Falieri, greatly alarmed and put out by the accident, wished the young man and his fit anywhere; and he carried his Annunciata, who hung her pretty head on her bosom and closed her eyes like a sick dove, himself up the steps into her own apartments in the interior of the Palace, although it was very hard work for him to do so.

Meanwhile the people, who had increased to crowds in the inner quadrangle, had been spectators of a remarkable scene. They were about to lift up the young man, whom they took to be quite dead, and carry him away, when an ugly old beggar-woman, all in rags, came limping up with a loud wail of grief; and punching their sides and ribs with her sharp elbows she made a way for herself through the thick of the crowd. When she at length saw the senseless youth, she cried, "Let him be, fools; you stupid people, let him be; he is not dead." Then she squatted down beside him; and taking his head in her lap she gently rubbed and stroked his forehead, calling him by the sweetest of names. As the people noted the old woman's ugly apish face, and the repulsive play of its muscles, bending over the young fellow's fine handsome face, his soft features now stiff and pale as in death, when they saw her filthy rags fluttering about over the rich clothing the young man wore, and her lean brownish-yellow arms and long hands trembling upon his forehead and exposed breast — they could not in truth resist shuddering with awe. It looked as if it were the grinning form of death himself in whose arms the young man lay. Hence the crowd standing round slipped away quietly one after the other, till there were only a few left They, when the young man opened his eyes with a deep sigh, took him up and carried him, at the old woman's request, to the Grand Canal, where a gondola took them both on board, the old woman and the youth, and brought them to the house which she had indicated as his dwelling. Need it be said that the young man was Antonio, and that the old woman was the beggar of the steps of the Franciscan Church, who wanted to make herself out to be his nurse?

When Antonio was quite recovered from his stupefaction and perceived the old woman at his bed-side, and knew that she had just been giving him some strengthening drops, he said brokenly in a hoarse voice, bending a long gloomy melancholy gaze upon her, "You with me, Margaret — that is good; what more faithful nurse could I have found than you? Oh! forgive me, mother, that I, a doltish, senseless boy, doubted for an instant what you discovered to me. Yes, you are the Margaret who reared me, who cared for me and tended me; I knew it all the time, but some evil spirit bewildered my thoughts. I have seen her; it is she — it is she. Did I not tell you there was some mysterious magical power dwelling in me, which exercised an uncontrollable supremacy over me? It has emerged from its obscurity dazzling with light, to effect my destruction through nameless joy. I now know all — everything. Was not my foster-father Bertuccio Nenolo, and did he not bring me up at his country-seat near Treviso?" "Yes, yes," replied the old woman, "it was indeed Bertuccio Nenolo, the great sea-captain, whom the sea devoured as he was about to adorn his temples with the victor's wreath." "Don't interrupt me," continued Antonio; "listen patiently to what I have to say.

"With Bertuccio Nenolo I lived in clover. I wore fine clothes; the table was always covered when I was hungry; and after I had said my three prayers properly I was allowed to run about the woods and fields just as I pleased. Close beside the villa there was a little wood of sweet pines, cool and dark, and filled with sweet scents and songs. There one evening, when the sun began to sink, I threw me down beneath a big tree, tired with running and jumping about, and stared up at the blue sky. Perhaps I was stupefied by the fragrant smell of the flowering herbs in the midst of which I lay; at any rate, my eyes closed involuntarily, and I sank into a state of dreamy reverie, from which I was awakened by a rustling, as if some one had struck a blow in the grass beside me. I started up into a sitting posture; an angelic child with heavenly eyes stood near me and looked down upon

51

me, smiling most sweetly and bewitchingly. 'O good boy,' she said, in a low soft voice, 'how beautiful and calmly you sleep, and yet death, nasty death, was so near to you.' Close beside my breast I saw a small black snake with its head crushed; the little girl had killed the poisonous reptile with a switch from a nut-tree, and just as it was wriggling on to my destruction. Then a trembling of sweet awe fell upon me; I knew that angels often came down from heaven above to rescue men in person from the threatening attack of some evil enemy. I fell upon my knees and raised my folded hands. 'Oh! you are surely an angel of light, sent by God to save my life,' I cried. The pretty creature stretched out both arms towards me and said softly, whilst a deeper flush mantled upon her cheeks, 'No, good boy; I am not an angel, but a girl — a child like you.' Then my feeling of awe gave place to a nameless delight, which spread like a gentle warmth through all my limbs. I rose to my feet; we clasped each other in our arms, our lips met, and we were speechless, weeping, sobbing with sweet unutterable sadness.

"Then a clear silvery voice cried through the wood, 'Annunciata! Annunciata!' 'I must go now, darling boy, mother is calling me,' whispered the little girl. My heart was rent with unspeakable pain. 'Oh! I love you so much,' I sobbed, and the scalding tears fell from the little girl's eyes upon my cheeks. 'I am so — so fond of you, good boy,' she cried, pressing a last kiss upon my lips. 'Annunciata,' the voice cried again; and the little girl disappeared behind the bushes. Now that, Margaret, was the moment when the mighty spark of love fell upon my soul, and it will gather strength, and, enkindling flame after flame, will continue to burn there for ever. A few days afterwards I was turned out of the house.

"Father Bluenose told me, since I did not cease talking about the lovely child who had appeared to me, and whose sweet voice I thought I heard in the rustling of the trees, in the gushing murmurs of the springs, and in the mysterious soughing of the sea — yes, then Father Bluenose told me that the girl could be none other than Nenolo's daughter Annunciata, who had come to the villa with her mother Francesca, but had left it again on the following day. O mother — Margaret — help me. Heaven! This Annunciata — is the Dogess." And Antonio buried his face in the pillows, weeping and sobbing with unspeakable emotion.

"My dear Tonino," said the old woman, "rouse yourself and be a man; come, do resist bravely this foolish emotion. Come, come, how can you think of despairing when you are in love? For whom does the golden flower of hope blossom if not for the lover? You do not know in the evening what the morning may bring; what you have beheld in your dreams comes to meet you in living form. The castle that hovered in the air stands all at once on the earth, a substantial and splendid building. See here, Tonino, you are not paying the least heed to my words; but my little finger tells me, and so does somebody else as well, that the bright standard of love is gaily waving for you out at sea. Patience, Tonino — patience, my boy!" Thus the old woman sought to comfort poor Antonio; and her words did really sound like sweet music.

He would not let her leave him again. The beggar-woman had disappeared from the steps of the Franciscan Church, and in her stead people saw Signor Antonio's housekeeper, dressed in becoming matronly style, limping about St. Mark's Square and buying the requisite provisions for his table.

Holy Thursday was come. It was to be celebrated on this occasion in more magnificent fashion than it had ever been before. In the middle of the Piazzetta of St. Mark's a high staging was erected for a special kind of artistic fire — something perfectly new, which was to be exhibited by a Greek — a man experienced in such matters. In the evening old Falieri came out on the balcony along with his beautiful lady, reflecting his pride and happiness in the magnificence of his surroundings, and with radiant eyes challenging all who stood near to admire and wonder. As he was about to take his seat on the chair of state he perceived Michele Steno actually on the same balcony with him, and saw that he had chosen a position whence he could keep his eyes constantly fixed upon the Dogess, and must of necessity be observed by her. Completely overmastered by furious rage, and wild with jealousy, Falieri shouted in a loud and commanding tone that Steno was to be at once removed from the balcony. Michele Steno raised his hand against Falieri, but that same moment the guards appeared, and compelled him to quit his place, which he did, foaming with rage and grinding his teeth, and threatening revenge in the most horrible imprecations.

Meanwhile Antonio, utterly beside himself at sight of his beloved Annunciata, had made his way out through the crowd, and was striding backwards and forwards in the darkness of the night alone along the edge of the sea, his heart rent by unutterable anguish. He debated within himself whether it would not be better to extinguish the consuming fire within him in the ice-cold waves than to be slowly tortured to death by hopeless pain. But little was wanting, and he had leapt into the sea; he was already standing on the last step that goes down to the water, when a voice called to him from a little boat, "Ay, a very good evening to you, Signor Antonio." By the reflection cast by the illuminations of the Square, he recognised that it was merry Pietro, one of his former comrades. He was standing in the boat, his new cap adorned with feathers and tinsel, and his new striped jacket gaily decorated with ribbons, whilst he held in his hand a large and beautiful nosegay of sweet-scented flowers. "Good evening, Pietro," shouted Antonio back, "what grand folks are you going to row to-night that you are decked off so fine?" "Oh!" replied Pietro, dancing till his boat rocked; "see you, Signor Antonio, I am going to earn my three sequins today; for I'm going to make the journey up to St. Mark's Tower and then down again, to take this nosegay to the beautiful Dogess." "But isn't that a risky and break-neck adventure, Pietro, my friend?" asked Antonio. "Well," he replied, "there is some little chance of breaking one's neck, especially as we go today right through the middle of the artificial fire. The Greek says, to be sure, that he has arranged everything so that the fire will not hurt a hair of anybody's head, but"——— Pietro shrugged his shoulders.

Antonio stepped down to Pietro in the boat, and now perceived that he stood close in front of the machine, which was fastened to a rope coming out of the sea. Other ropes, by means of which the machine was to be drawn up, were lost in the night. "Now listen, Pietro," began Antonio, after a silent pause, "see here, comrade, if you could earn ten sequins today without exposing your life to danger, would it not be more agreeable to you?" "Why, of course," and Pietro burst into a good hearty laugh. "Well then," continued Antonio, "take these ten sequins and change clothes with me, and let me take your place, I will go up instead of you. Do, my good friend and comrade, Pietro, let me go up." Pietro shook his head dubiously, and weighing the money in his hand, said, "You are very kind, Signor Antonio, to still call a poor devil like me your comrade, and you are generous as well. The money I should certainly like very much; but, on the other hand, to place this nosegay in our beautiful Dogess's hand myself, to hear her sweet voice — and after all that's really why I am ready to risk my life. Well, since it is you, Signor Antonio, I close with your offer." They both hastily changed their clothes; and hardly was Antonio dressed when Pietro cried, "Quick, into the machine; the signal is given." At the same moment the sea was lit up with the reflection of thousands of bright flashes, and all the air along the margin of the sea rang with loud reverberating thunders. Right through the midst of the hissing crackling flames of the artificial fire, Antonio rose up into the air with the speed of a hurricane, and shot down uninjured upon the balcony, hovering in front of the

56

Dogess. She had risen to her feet and stepped forward; he felt her breath on his cheeks; he gave her the nosegay. But in the unspeakable delirious delight of the moment he was clasped as if in red-hot arms by the fiery pain of hopeless love. Senseless, insane with longing, rapture, anguish, he grasped her hand, and covered it with burning kisses, crying in the sharp tone of despairing misery, "O Annunciata!" Then the machine, like a blind instrument of fate, whisked him away from his beloved back to the sea, where he sank down stunned, quite exhausted, into Pietro's arms, who was waiting for him in the boat.

Meanwhile the Doge's balcony was the scene of tumult and confusion. A small strip of paper had been found fastened to the Doge's seat, containing in the common Venetian dialect the words:

Il Dose Falier della bella muier,

I altri la gode é lui la mantien.

(The Doge Falieri, the husband of the beautiful lady; others kiss her, and he — he keeps her.)

Old Falieri burst into a violent fit of passion, and swore that the severest punishment should overtake the man who had been guilty of this audacious offence. As he cast his eyes about they fell upon Michele Steno standing beneath the balcony in the Square, in the full light of the torches; he at once commanded his guards to arrest him as the instigator of the outrage. This command of the Doge's provoked a universal cry of dissent; in giving way to his overmastering rage he was offering insult to both Seignory and populace, violating the rights of the former, and spoiling the latter's enjoyment of their holiday. The members of the Seignory left their places; but old Marino Bodoeri mixed among the people, actively representing the grave nature of the outrage that had been done to the head of the state, and seeking to direct the popular hatred upon Michele Steno. Nor had Falieri judged wrongly; for Michele Steno, on being expelled from the Duke's balcony, had really hurried off home, and there written the above-mentioned slanderous words; then when all eyes were fixed upon the artificial fire, he had fastened the strip of paper to the Doge's seat, and withdrawn from the gallery again unobserved. He maliciously hoped it would be a galling blow for them, for both the Doge and the Dogess, and that the wound would rankle deeply — so deeply as to touch a vital part. Willingly and openly he admitted the deed, and transferred all blame to the Doge, since he had been the first to give umbrage to him.

The Seignory had been for some time dissatisfied with their chief, for instead of meeting the just expectations of the state, he gave proofs daily that the fiery warlike courage in his frozen and worn-out heart was merely like the artificial fire which bursts with a furious rush out of the rocket-apparatus, but immediately disappears in black lifeless flakes, and has accomplished nothing. Moreover, since his union with his young and beautiful wife (it had long before leaked out that he was married to her directly after attaining to the Dogate) old Falieri's jealousy no longer let him appear in the character of heroic captain, but rather of vechio Pantalone (old fool); hence it was that the Seignory, nursing their swelling resentment, were more inclined to condone Michele Steno's fault, than to see justice done to their deeply-wounded chief. The matter was referred by the Council of Ten to the Forty, one of the leaders of which Michele had formerly been. The verdict was that Michele Steno had already suffered sufficiently, and a month's banishment was quite punishment enough for the offence. This sentence only served to feed anew and more fully old Falieri's bitterness against a Seignory which, instead of protecting their own head, had the impudence to punish insults that were offered to him as they would offences of merely the most insignificant description.

As generally happens in the case of lovers, once a single ray of the happiness of love has fallen upon them, they are surrounded for days and weeks and months by a sort of golden veil, and dream dreams of Paradise; and so Antonio could not recover himself from the stupefying rapture of that happy moment; he could hardly breathe for delirious sadness. He had been well scolded by the old woman for running such a great risk; and she never ceased mumbling and grumbling about exposure to unnecessary danger.

But one day she came hopping and dancing with her staff in the strange way she had when apparently affected by some foreign magical influence. Without heeding Antonio's words and questions, she began to chuckle and laugh, and kindling a small fire in the stove, she put a little pan on it, into which she poured several ingredients from many various-coloured phials, and made a salve, which she put into a little box; then she limped out of the house again, chuckling and laughing. She did not return until late at night, when she sat down in the easy-chair, panting and coughing for breath; and after she had in a measure recovered from her great exhaustion, she at length began, "Tonino, my boy Tonino, whom do you think I have come from? See — try if you can guess. Whom do I come from? where have I been?" Antonio looked at her, and a singular instinctive feeling took possession of him. "Well now," chuckled the old woman, "I have come from her — her herself, from the pretty dove, lovely Annunciata." "Don't drive me mad, old woman!" shouted Antonio. "What do you say?" continued she, "I am always thinking about you, my Tonino.

"This morning, whilst I was haggling for some fine fruit under the peristyle of the Palace, I heard the people talking with bated breath of the accident that had befallen the beautiful Dogess. I inquired again and again of several people, and at last a big, uncultivated, red haired fellow, who stood leaning against a column, yawning and chawing lemons, said to me, 'Oh well, a young scorpion has been trying its little teeth on the little finger of her left hand, and there's been a drop or two of blood shed — that's all. My master, Signor Doctor Giovanni Basseggio, is now in the palace, and he has, no doubt, before this cut off her pretty hand, and the finger with it.' Just as the fellow was telling me this there arose a great noise on the broad steps, and a little man — such a tiny little man — came rolling down at our feet, screaming and lamenting, for the guards had kicked him down as if he had

60

been a nine pin. The people gathered round him, laughing heartily; the little man struggled and fought with his legs in the air without being able to get up; but the red-haired fellow rushed forward, snatched up the little doctor, tucked him under his arm, and ran off with him as fast as his legs could carry him to the Canal, where he got into a gondola with him and rowed away — the little doctor screaming and yelling with all his might the whole time. I knew how it was; just as Signor Basseggio was getting his knife ready to cut off the pretty hand, the Doge had had him kicked down the steps. I also thought of something else — quick — quick as you can — go home make a salve — and then come back here to the Ducal Palace.

"And I stood on the great stairs with my bright little phial in my hand. Old Falieri was just coming down; he darted a glance at me, and, his choler rising, said, 'What does this old woman want here?' Then I curtsied low — quite down to the ground — as well as I could, and told him that I had a nice remedy which would very soon cure the beautiful Dogess. When the old man heard that, he fixed a terrible keen look upon me, and stroked his grey beard into order; then he seized me by both shoulders and pushed me upstairs and on into the chamber, where I nearly fell all my length. O Tonino, there was the pretty child reclining on a couch, as pale as death, sighing and moaning with pain and softly lamenting, 'Oh! I am poisoned in every vein.' But I at once set to work and took off the simple doctor's silly plaster. O just Heaven! her dear little hand — all red as red — and swollen. Well, well, my salve cooled it — soothed it. 'That does it good; yes, that does it good,' softly whispered the sick darling. Then Marino cried quite delighted, 'You shall have a thousand sequins, old woman, if you save me the Dogess;' and therewith he left the room.

"For three hours I sat there, holding her little hand in mine, stroking and attending to it. Then the darling woman woke up out of the gentle slumber into which she had fallen, and no longer felt any pain. After I had made a fresh poultice, she looked at me with eyes brimming with gladness. Then I said, 'O most noble lady, you once saved a boy's life when you killed the little snake that was about to attack him as he slept.' O Tonino, you should have seen the hot blood rush into her pale face, as if a ray of the setting sun had fallen upon it — and how her eyes flashed with the fire of joy. 'Oh! yes, old woman,' she said, 'oh! I was quite a child then — it was at my father's country villa. Oh! he was a dear pretty boy — I often think of him now. I don't think I have ever had a single happy experience since that time.' Then I began to talk about you, that you were in Venice, that your heart still beat with the love and rapture of that moment, that, in order to gaze once more in the heavenly eyes of the angel who saved you, you had faced the risk of the dangerous aerial voyage, that you it was who had given her the nosegay on Holy Thursday. 'O Tonino, Tonino,' she cried in an ecstasy of delight, 'I felt it, I felt it; when he pressed my hand to his lips, when he named my name, I could not conceive why it went so strangely to my heart; it was indeed pleasure, but pain as well. Bring him here, bring him to me — the pretty boy.'" As the old woman said this Antonio threw himself upon his knees and cried like one insane, "O good God! pray let no dire fate overtake me now — now at least until I have seen her, have pressed her to my heart." He wanted the old woman to take him to the Palace the very next day; but she flatly refused, since old Falieri was in the habit of paying visits to his sick wife nearly every hour that came.

Several days went by; the old woman had completely cured the Dogess; but as yet it had been quite impossible to take Antonio to see her. The old woman soothed his impatience as well as she could, always repeating that she was constantly talking to beautiful Annunciata about the Antonio whose life she had saved, and who loved her so passionately. Tormented by all the pangs of desire and yearning love, Antonio spent his time in going about in his gondola and restlessly traversing the squares. But his footsteps involuntarily turned time after time in the direction of the Ducal Palace. One day he saw Pietro standing on the bridge close to the back part of the Palace, opposite the prisons, leaning on a gay-coloured oar, whilst a gondola, fastened to one of the pillars, was rocking on the Canal. Although small, it had a comfortable little deck, was adorned with tasteful carvings, and even decorated with the Venetian flag, so that it bore some resemblance to the Bucentaur. As soon as Pietro saw his former comrade he shouted out to him, "Hi! Signor Antonio, the best of good greetings to you; your sequins have brought me good luck." Antonio asked somewhat absently what sort of good luck he meant, and learned the important intelligence that nearly every evening Pietro had to take the Doge and Dogess in his gondola across to Giudecca, where the Doge had a nice house not far from San Giorgio Maggiore. Antonio stared at Pietro, and then burst out spasmodically, "Comrade, you may earn another ten sequins and more if you like. Let me take your place; I will row the Doge over." But Pietro informed him that he could not think of doing so, for the Doge knew him and would not trust himself with anybody else. At length when Antonio, his mind excited by all the tortures of love, began to give way to unbridled anger, and violently importune him, and to swear in an insane and ridiculous fashion that he would leap after the gondola and drag it down under the sea, Pietro replied laughing, "Why, Signor Antonio, Signor Antonio, why, I declare you have quite lost yourself in the Dogess's beautiful eyes." But he consented to allow Antonio to go with him as his assistant in rowing; he would excuse it to old Falieri on the ground of the weight of the boat, as well, as being himself a little weak and unwell, and old Falieri did always think the gondola went too slowly on this trip. Off Antonio ran, and he only just returned to the bridge in time, dressed in coarse oarsman's clothing, his face stained, and with a long moustache stuck above his lips, for the Doge came down from the Palace with the Dogess, both attired most splendidly and magnificently. "Who's that stranger fellow there?" began the Doge angrily to Pietro; and it required all Pietro's most solemn asseverations that he really required an assistant, before the old man could be induced to allow Antonio to help row the gondola.

It often happens that in the midst of the wildest delirium of delight and rapture the soul, strengthened as it were by the power of the moment, is able to impose fetters upon itself, and to control the flames of passion which threaten to blaze out from the heart. In a similar way Antonio, albeit he was close beside the lovely Annunciata and the seam of her dress touched him, was able to hide his consuming passion by maintaining a firm and powerful hold upon his oar, and, whilst avoiding any greater risk, by only glancing at her momentarily now and then. Old Falieri was all smirks and smiles; he kissed and fondled beautiful Annunciata's little white hands, and threw his arm around her slender waist. In the middle of the channel, when St. Mark's Square and magnificent Venice with all her proud towers and palaces lay extended before them, old Falieri raised his head and said, gazing proudly about him, "Now, my darling, is it not a grand thing to ride on the sea with the lord — the husband of the sea? Yes, my darling, don't be jealous of my bride, who is submissively bearing us on her broad bosom. Listen to the gentle splashing of the wavelets; are they not words of love which she is whispering to the husband who rules her? Yes, yes, my darling, you indeed wear my ring on your finger, but she below guards in the depths of her bosom the ring of betrothal which I threw to her." "Oh! my princely Sir," began Annunciata, "oh! how can this cold treacherous water be your bride? it quite makes me shiver to think that you are married to this proud imperious element." Old Falieri laughed till his chin and beard tottered and shook. "Don't distress yourself, my pet," he said, "it's far better, of course, to rest in your soft warm arms than in the ice-cold lap of my bride below there; but it's a grand thing to ride on the sea with the lord of the sea!" Just as the Doge was saying these words, the faint strains of music at a distance came floating towards them. The notes of a soft male voice, gliding along the waves of the sea, came nearer and nearer; the words that were sung were —

Ah! senza amare,
Andare sul mare,
Col sposo del' mare
Non puo consolare.

Other voices took up the strain, and the same words were repeated again and again in every-varying alternation, until the song died away like the soft breath of the wind as it were. Old Falieri appeared not to pay the slightest heed to the song; on the contrary, he was relating to the Dogess with much prolixity the meaning and history of the solemnity which takes place on Ascension Day when the Doge throws his ring from the Bucentaur and is married to the sea.

He spoke of the victories of the republic, and how she had formerly conquered Istria and Dalmatia under the rule of Peter Urseolus the Second,24 and how this ceremony had its origin in that conquest But if old Falieri heeded not the song, so now his tales were lost upon the Dogess. She sat with her mind completely wrapped up in the sweet sounds which came floating along the sea. When the song came to an end her eyes wore a strange far-off look, as if she were awakening from a profound dream and striving to see and interpret the images which sportively mocked her efforts to hold them fast. "Senza amare, senza amare, non puo consolare," she whispered softly, whilst the tears glistened like bright pearls in her heavenly eyes, and sighs escaped her breast as it heaved and sank with the violence of her emotions. Still smirking and smiling and talking away, the old man, with the Dogess at his side, stepped out upon the balcony of his house near San Giorgio Maggiore, without noticing that Annunciata stood at his side like one in a dream, speechless, her tearful eyes fixed upon some far-off land, whilst her heart was agitated by feelings of a singular and mysterious character. A young man in gondolier's costume blew a blast on a conch-shaped horn, till the sounds echoed far away over the sea. At this signal another gondola drew near. Meanwhile an attendant bearing a sunshade and a maid had approached the Doge and Dogess; and thus attended they went towards the palace. The second gondola came to shore, and from it stepped forth Marino Bodoeri and several other persons, amongst whom were merchants, artists, nay people out of the lowest classes of the populace even; and they followed the Doge.

Antonio could hardly wait until the following evening, since he hoped then to have the desired message from his beloved Annunciata. At last — at last the old woman came limping in, dropped panting into the arm-chair, and clapped her thin bony hands together again and again, crying. "Tonino, O Tonino! what in the world has happened to our dear darling? When I went into her room, there she lay on the couch with her eyes half closed, her pretty head resting on her arm, neither slumbering nor awake, neither sick nor well. I approached her: 'Oh! noble lady,' said I, 'what misfortune has happened to you? Does your scarce-healed wound hurt you still?' But she looked at me, oh! with such eyes, Antonio — I have never seen anything like them. And directly I looked down into the humid moonlight that was in them, they withdrew behind the dark clouds of their silken lashes. Then sighing a sigh that came from the depths of her heart, she turned her lovely pale face to the wall and whispered softly — so softly, but oh! so sadly! that I was cut right to the heart, 'Amare — amare — ah! senza amare! ' I fetched a little chair and sat down beside her, and began to talk about you. She buried herself in the cushions; and her breathing, coming quicker and quicker and quicker, turned to sighing. I told her candidly that you had been in the gondola disguised, and that I would now at once without delay take you, who were dying of love and longing, to see her. Then she suddenly started up from the cushions, and whilst the scalding tears streamed down her cheeks, she exclaimed vehemently, 'For God's sake! By all the Holy Saints! no — no — I cannot see him, old woman. I conjure you, tell him he is never — never again to come near me — never. Tell him he is to leave Venice, to go away at once!' 'So then you will let my poor Antonio die?' I interposed. Then she sank back upon the cushions, apparently smarting from the most unutterable anguish, and her voice was almost choked with tears as she sobbed out, 'Shall not I also die the bitterest of deaths?' At this point old Falieri entered the room, and at a sign from him I had to withdraw." "She has rejected me — away — away into the sea!" cried Antonio, giving way to utter despair. The old woman chuckled and laughed in her usual way, and went on, "You simple child! you simple child! don't you see that lovely Annunciata loves you with all the intensity, with all the agonised love of which a woman's heart is capable? You simple boy! Late tomorrow evening slip into the Ducal Palace; you will find me in the second gallery on the right from the great staircase, and then we will see what's to be done."

The following evening as Antonio, trembling with expectant happiness, stole up the great staircase, his conscience suddenly smote him, as though he were about to commit some great crime. He was so dazed, and he trembled and shook so, that he was scarcely able to climb the stairs. He had to stop and rest by leaning himself against a column immediately in front of the gallery that had been indicated to him. All at once he was plunged in the midst of a bright glare of torches, and before he could move from the place old Bodoeri stood in front of him, accompanied by some servants, who bore the torches. Bodoeri fixed his eyes upon the young man, and then said, "Ha! you are Antonio; you have been assigned this post, I know; come, follow me." Antonio, convinced that his proposed interview with the

Dogess was betrayed, followed, not without trembling. But imagine his astonishment when, on entering a remote room, Bodoeri embraced him and spoke of the importance of the post that had been assigned to him, and which he would have to maintain with courage and firm resolution that very night. But his amazement increased to anxious fear and dismay when he learned that a conspiracy had been long ripening against the Seignory, and that at the head of it was the Doge himself. And this was the night in which, agreeably to the resolutions come to in Falieri's house on Giudecca, the Seignory was to fall and old Marino Falieri was to be proclaimed sovereign Duke of Venice.

Antonio stared at Bodoeri without uttering a word; Bodoeri interpreted the young man's silence as a refusal to take part in the execution of the formidable conspiracy, and he cried incensed, "You cowardly fool! You shall not leave this palace again; you shall either take up arms on our side or die — but talk to this man first" A tall and noble figure stepped forward from the dark background of the apartment. As soon as Antonio saw the man's face, which he could not do until he came into the light of the torches, and recognised it, he threw himself upon his knees and cried, completely losing his presence of mind at seeing him whom he never dreamt of seeing again, "O good God! my father, Bertuccio Nenolo! my dear foster-parent." Nenolo raised the young man up, clasped him in his arms, and said in a gentle voice, "Aye, of a verity I am Bertuccio Nenolo, whom you perhaps thought lay buried at the bottom of the sea, but I have only quite recently escaped from my shameful captivity at the hands of the savage Morbassan. Yes, I am the Bertuccio Nanolo who adopted you. And I never for a moment dreamt that the stupid servants whom Bodoeri sent to take possession of the villa, which he had bought of me, would turn you out of the house. You infatuated youth! Do you hesitate to take up arms against a despotic caste whose cruelty robbed you of a father? Ay! go down to the quadrangle of the Fontego, and the stains which you will there see on the stone pavements are the stains of your father's blood. The Seignory when making over to the German merchants the dépôt and exchange which you know under the name of the Fontego, forbade all those who had offices assigned to them to take the keys with them when they went away; they were to leave them with the official in charge of the Fontego. Your father acted contrary to this law, and had therefore incurred a heavy penalty. But now when the offices were opened on your father's return, there was found amongst his wares a chest of false Venetian coins. He vainly protested his innocence; it was only too evident that some malicious fiend, perhaps the official in charge himself, had smuggled in the chest in order to ruin your father. The inexorable judges, satisfied that the chest had been found in your father's offices, condemned him to death. He was executed in the quadrangle of the Fontego; nor would you now be living if faithful Margaret had not saved you. I, your father's truest friend, adopted you; and in order that you might not betray yourself to the Seignory, you were not told what was your father's name. But now — now, Anthony

Dalbirger,— now is the time — now, to seize your arms and revenge upon the heads of the Seignory your father's shameful death."

Antonio, fired by the spirit of vengeance, swore to be true to the conspirators and to act with invincible courage. It is well known that it was the affront put upon Bertuccio Nenolo by Dandulo when he was appointed to superintend the naval preparations, and on the occasion of a quarrel struck Nenolo in the face, that induced him to join with his ambitious son-inlaw in his conspiracy against the Seignory. Both Nenolo and Bodoeri were desirous for old Falieri to assume the princely mantle in order that they might themselves rise along with him. The conspirators' plan was to spread abroad the news that the Genoese fleet lay before the Lagune. Then when night came the great bell in St. Mark's Tower was to be rung, and the town summoned to arms, under the false pretext of defence. This was to be the signal for the conspirators, whose numbers were considerable, and who were scattered throughout all Venice, to occupy St. Mark's Square, make themselves masters of the remaining principal squares of the town, murder the leading men of the Seignory, and proclaim the Doge sovereign Duke of Venice.

But it was not the will of Heaven that this murderous scheme should succeed, nor that the fundamental constitution of the harassed state should be trampled in the dust by old Falieri — a man inflamed with pride and haughtiness. The meetings in Falieri's house on Giudecca had not escaped the watchfulness of the Ten; but they failed altogether to learn any reliable intelligence. But the conscience of one of the conspirators, a fur-merchant of Pisa, Bentian by name, pricked him; he resolved to save from destruction his friend and gossip, Nicolas Leoni, a member of the Council of Ten. When twilight came on, he went to him and besought him not to leave his house during the night, no matter what occurred. Leoni's suspicion was aroused; he detained the fur-merchant, and on pressing him closely learned the whole scheme. In conjunction with Giovanni Gradenigo and Marco Cornaro he called the Council of Ten together in St. Salvador's (church); and there, in less than three hours, measures were taken calculated to stifle all the efforts of the conspirators on the first sign of movement.

Antonio's commission was to take a body of men and go to St. Mark's Tower, and see that the bell was tolled. Arrived there, he found the tower occupied by a large force of Arsenal troops, who, on his attempting to approach, charged upon him with their halberds. His own band, seized with a sudden panic, scattered like chaff; and he himself slipped away in the darkness of the night. But he heard the footsteps of a man following close at his heels; he felt him lay hands upon him, and he was just on the point of cutting his pursuer down when by means of a sudden flash of light he recognised Pietro. "Save yourself," cried he, "save yourself, Antonio,— here in my gondola. All is betrayed. Bodoeri — Nenolo — are in the power of the Seignory; the doors of the Ducal Palace are closed; the Doge is confined a prisoner in his own apartment — watched like a criminal by his own faithless guards. Come along — make haste — get away." Almost stupefied, Antonio suffered himself to be dragged into the gondola. Muffled voices — the clash of weapons — single cries for help — then with the deepest blackness of the night there followed a breathless awful silence. Next morning the populace, stricken with terror, beheld a fearful sight; it made every man's blood run cold in his veins. The Council of the Ten had that very same night passed sentence of death upon the leaders of the conspiracy who had been seized. They were strangled, and suspended from the balcony at the side of the Palace overlooking the Piazzetta, the one whence the Doge was in the habit of witnessing all ceremonies,— and where, alas! Antonio had hovered in the air before the lovely Annunciata, and where she had received from him the nosegay of flowers. Amongst the corpses were those of Marino Bodoeri and Bertuccio Nenolo. Two days later old Marino Falieri was sentenced to death by the Council of Ten, and executed on the so-called Giant Stairs of the Palace.

Antonio wandered about unconsciously, like a man in a dream; no one laid hands upon him, for no one recognised him as having been of the number of the conspirators. On seeing old Falieri's grey head fall, he started up, as it were, out of his death-like trance. With a most unearthly scream — with the shout, "Annunciata!" he rushed storming in the Palace, and along the passages. Nobody stopped him; the guards, as if stupefied by the terrible thing that had just taken place, only stared after him. The old crone came to meet him, loudly lamenting and complaining; she seized his hand and — a few steps more, and along with her he entered Annunciata's room. There she lay, poor thing, on the couch, as if already dead. Antonio rushed towards her and covered her hands with burning kisses, calling her by the sweetest and tenderest names.

Then she slowly opened her lovely heavenly eyes and saw Antonio; at first, however, it appeared as if it cost her an effort to call him to mind; but speedily she raised herself up, threw both her arms around his neck, and drew him to her bosom, showering down her hot tears upon him and kissing his cheeks — his lips. "Antonio — my Antonio — I love you, oh! more than I can tell you — yes, yes, there is a heaven on earth. What are my father's and my uncle's and my husband's death in comparison with the blissful joy of your love? Oh! let us flee — flee from this scene of blood and murder." Thus spake Annunciata, her heart rent by the bitterest anguish, as well as by the most passionate love. Amid thousands of kisses and never-ending tears, the two lovers mutually swore eternal fidelity; and, forgetting the fearful events of the terrible day that was past, they turned their eyes from the earth and looked up into the heaven which the spirit of love had unfolded to their view. The old woman advised them to flee to Chiozza; thence Antonio intended to travel in an opposite direction by land towards his own native country.

His friend, Pietro, procured him a small boat and had it brought to the bridge behind the Palace. When night came, Annunciata, enveloped in a thick shawl, crept stealthily down the steps with her lover, attended by old Margaret, who bore some valuable jewel caskets in her hood. They reached the bridge unobserved, and unobserved they embarked in their small craft. Antonio seized the oar, and away they went at a quick and vigorous rate. The bright moonlight danced along the waves in front of them like a gladsome messenger of love. They reached the open sea. Then began a peculiar whistling and howling of the wind far above their heads; black shadows came trooping up and hung themselves like a dark veil over the bright face of the moon. The dancing moonshine, the gladsome messenger of love, sank in the black depths of the sea amongst its muttering thunders. The storm came on and drove the black piled-up masses of clouds in front of it with wrathful violence. Up and down tossed the boat. "O help us! God, help us!" screamed the old woman. Antonio, no longer master of the oar, clasped his darling Annunciata in his arms, whilst she, aroused by his fiery kisses, strained him to her bosom in the intensity of her rapturous affection. "O my Antonio!"—"O my Annunciata!" they whispered, heedless of the storm which raged and blustered ever more furiously. Then the sea, the jealous widow of the beheaded Doge Falieri, stretched up her foaming waves as if they were giant arms, and seized upon the lovers, and dragged them, along with the old woman, down, down into her fathomless depths.

As soon as the man in the mantle had thus concluded his narrative, he jumped up quickly and left the room with strong rapid strides. The friends followed him with their eyes, silently and very much astonished; then they went to take another look at the picture. The old Doge again looked down upon them with a smirk, in his ridiculous finery and foppish vanity; but when they carefully looked into the Dogess's face they perceived quite plainly that the shadow of some unknown pain — a pain of which she only had a foreboding — was throned upon her lily brow, and that dreamy aspirations of love gleamed from behind her dark lashes, and hovered around her sweet lips. The Hostile Power seemed to be threatening death and destruction from out the distant sea and the vaporous clouds which enshrouded St. Mark's. They now had a clear conception of the deeper significance of the charming picture; but so often as they looked upon it again, all the sympathetic sorrow which they had felt at the history of Antonio and Annunciata's love returned upon them and filled the deepest recesses of their souls with its pleasurable awe.

# Footnotes

1 Written for the Taschenbuch der Liebe und Freundschaft gewidmet, 1819; edited by S. Schütze, Frankfort-on-Main.

2 C W. Kolbe, junr., historical and genre painter, was born in 1781 and died in 1853.

3 The story Turandot has a history. Its prototype is in the Persian poet Nizámí (1141–1203). From Gozzi it was translated into German by Werthes; and it was from his translation that Schiller worked up his play in November and December, 1801. The proud Turandot, daughter of the Emperor of China, entertains such loathing of marriage that she rejects all suitors, until on her father's threatening to compel her to wed, she institutes a kind of version of the caskets in the Merchant of Venice. Any prince may woo for her, but in a peculiar way. He must solve three riddles in the full assembly of the court. If he succeeds, he wins the princess; if he does not succeed, he loses his own head. In Gozzi the three riddles are about the Year, the Sun, and (extremely inapposite to the circumstances) the Lion of the Adriatic. The two last Schiller replaced by riddles about the Eye and the Plough.

4 Calaf, Prince of Astrakhan, successfully solves the riddles and wins the Princess Turandot.

5 The story of this Doge's conspiracy has furnished materials for a tragedy to Byron (1821), Casimir Delavinge (1829), and Albert Lindner (1875). A translation of the story

is given by Mr. F. Cohen (Sir F. Palgrave) from Sanuto's Chronicle, in the Appendix to the play in Byron's works.

6 Paganino Dona, one of the greatest of Genoese admirals, took and burnt Parenzo, a town on the west coast of Istria, on the 11th of August, 1354. At this period the rivalry between the two republics, Venice and Genoa, in their commercial relations with the East and in the Black Sea, was especially bitter, and they were almost constantly at war with each other.

7 Andrea Dandolo (1307–1354), Doge from 1343 to 1354. During his reign Venice actively extended her commercial conquests in the Black Sea and the countries around the Levant, engaged part of the time in active hostilities with the Genoese.

8 The sequin was a gold coin of Venice and Tuscany, worth about 9s. 3d. It is sometimes used as equivalent to ducat.

9 Pope Innocent VI., Pope at Avignon, from 1352 to 1362.

10 Hoffmann states that he derived his materials for this story from Le Bret's "History of Venice,"— a book which, unfortunately, up to the time of going to press, the translator had not been able to obtain.

11 Nicolo Pisani, a very active naval commander in the third war with Genoa (1350–1355), fought battles in the Bosphorus, off Sardinia, and at Porto Longo, near Modon (Greece).

12 Sardinia was for many, many years an object of

contention between Pisa, Genoa, and the Aragonese. At this time (1354) it belonged to the latter, but the Genoese were constantly endeavouring to stir up the people of the island to revolt against the Aragonese; hence we may see reason for Pisani's being in Sardinian waters.

13 Equivalent to "Governor," Chioggia was an old town thirty miles south of Venice, at the southern extremity of the Lagune. Chiozza = Chioggia.

14 The state barge of Venice; the word means "little golden boat." Pope Alexander III. bestowed upon the Doge Sebastian Ziani, for his victory over Frederick Barbarossa near Parenzo on Ascension Day, 1177, a ring in token of the suzerainty of Venice over the Adriatic. From this time dates the observance of the annual ceremony of the Doge's marrying the Adriatic from the Bucentaur.

15 San Giorgio Maggiore. Venice, as everybody knows, is not built upon the mainland but upon islands. The two largest, whose greatest length is from east to west, are divided by the Grand Canal, upon which axe situated most of the palaces and important public buildings. South of these two principal islands, and separated from them by the Giudecca Canal, are the islands of Giudecca and San Giorgio Maggiore close together, the latter on the east and opposite the south entrance to the Grand Canal, beyond which are the Piazetta and St. Mark's Square.

16 This is larger than the gondola, and also more modern; it is calculated to hold six persons, and even luggage.

17 The Fondaco de' Tedeschi, erected in 1506, on the

Grand Canal. It was formerly decorated externally with paintings by Titian and his pupils. At first it served as dépôt for the wares of German merchants (whence its name), but is now used as a custom-house.

18 Louis I. the Great of Hungary (1342–1382). The Dalmatian and Istrian sea-board formed a fruitful source of contention between the Venetians and Hungary, Louis proving a very formidable opponent to the Republic.

19 At this epoch Venice was the mart and mediatory between the West and the East, the commercial riches of the latter having been opened up to the feudal civilisation of Europe, chiefly through the Crusades. Hence the cosmopolitan character of the merchants on the Rialto.

20 In the year 1348, Venice was visited by an earthquake, and this was followed by the plague (the Black Death). In order to complete the roll of the republic's misfortunes in this gloomy year, it may be added that she also lost almost the whole of her Black Sea fleet to the Genoese.

21 It may perhaps be interesting to observe that a precisely similar occurrence forms the central feature in H. v. Kleist's "Erdbeben in Chili" (1810), perhaps one of the best of his short stories.

22 Narrated in the translation of the Chronicle of Sanuto by Sir Francis Palgrave in Byron's notes to "Marino Faliero."

23 On the island of Sapenzia, south-west of the Morea.

24 Pietro Urseolo I. was Doge from 991 to 1009; Dalmatia was subdued in 997.